The Water in our Veins

Penn Stewart

Acknowledgements

"Bound" Dogzplot;
"The Weight on my Back" Pacifica Literary Review;
"Finale" Union Station Magazine; and
"No Safe Harbor" Literary Orphans.

Contents

Bound

It's daybreak and we're just outside of Memphis. The baby's breathing is like raspy road noise. Oncoming headlights pierce the fog and spread like spilled milk on the wet windshield. You stir in your seat, fighting a nightmare or reality. You told me he wasn't mine and I wanted to believe you, to be free from it all. But yoeeeu called last night— needing a ride to Saint Jude's—and I knew you had lied.

Steel girders carry us over the Mississippi, taillights flash red and traffic stops. We're caught between two states and the currents churn in the murky waters beneath us. Trucks and cars idle; exhaust pumps into the fog and wraps us in toxic fumes. He coughs. I turn to check on him.

From here, we'll have to crawl forward.

"It feels like saltwater in my veins," Layla says. "Cold and gritty."

I hold her other hand, the one not attached to the arm with the IV drip. "Did you know the salinity of ocean water and our blood is the same?"

"You've told me that before, but I don't think it's true." She squeezes the rubber ball in her other hand.

"I read it somewhere."

"I think it's one of those things that sounds good, but it's not really true."

I want to say, How'd you get so smart? Layla has always been one step ahead of us, the kind of child that lets you see the world in a new way. "She's nine going on fifty," we say when describing her to new acquaintances who ask if Karen and I have any kids. I look over at the IV bag. "Only 200ml left."

She glances up. Too quickly to read the markers on the side of the bag, but enough to show me she's listening. Her hand pumps the ball like it's her own heart, each squeeze another pulse, another push, each one determined but never desperate.

When Layla was born, our friends teased us about having a "change of life baby." Karen and I were married for ten years before she came along. I'm sure our friends thought we would never have children, but we wanted to wait until things settled a bit before having a kid. We should've known better; life never settles down.

On the television mounted up in the corner of the room, CNN reports an airliner was shot down by a surface to air missile over the Ukraine. The missile, they say, contained an explosive core surrounded by two mantles containing mine fragments. These fragments were in the shape of cubes or bowties and penetrated the aircraft when it was triggered by a proximity fuse. The Boeing 777 carried nearly 300 people and none survived. I look around for the remote and wonder why anyone would leave CNN on in this setting. It seems the barrage of catastrophes—mass shootings, mudslides consuming villages, ships lost at sea—are the last thing someone enduring treatment would want to watch.

On the way home, Layla runs her fingers

through her hair. "Hair loss is likely," Dr. Bridges had said when we discussed treatments. We stop by A Stich in Time, a sewing shop near our home and wander among the bolts of fabric. Her fingertips trace designs and she uses the back of her hand to test suppleness. She doesn't seem to find anything she likes, and her hands drift back to her hair flowing over her shoulders. "Can't find anything?" I ask.

She shrugs and meanders off on her own. Her tenth birthday is less than a month away, and I've thought about what to give her. Every time I think of a DVD, a game, a cute plushy, a book she's mentioned, it falls flat and I imagine the disappointment on her face. On one hand, I know she'll be gracious and thank me for whatever it is she unwraps, but on the other hand, I know the only thing she wishes for is something I cannot give. She decides on a hot pink furry fabric that looks like hair for a Sesame Street Muppet.

Her hand runs over it, smoothing the fabric one way, and then pushes it back the other way so it stands tall and then folds it over her fist, as if it's a little head. "This is what your hair looks like when you wake up in the morning," she says with a grin.

"Well at least it's not pink," I say.

"Yeah, fuchsia wouldn't work with your skin tone. You're an autumn."

I am an autumn. I'm not sure what she means, but I feel the gentle shift of age, the change of seasons from summer to fall in my essence. The slowing of my reflexes, the aches in knees once springy and nimble on the basketball court. Greying temples never bothered me, but the subtle sag of skin under my chin—a reminder of my own mortality— crept up and caught me by surprise. My daughter is a spring, too young for her leaves to be falling.

Last summer, before the diagnosis, we were in a swimming pool and Layla attached herself to my back. "I'm a barnacle," she proclaimed. I burbled into the water, making a motorboat noise with my lips, and pushed off the side and ferried her to the shallow end. Her breath and giggles in my ear. I swam the length of the pool with her arms around my neck, pushing harder, each stroke defined as her weight slowed me down. I hadn't expected to struggle.

We leave the fabric store and drive home, her purchase sits on her lap with one hand hidden in the bag. "I'm going to make a hat like DJ Lance Rock," she says.

"That'll be fun." I Remember Yo Gaba Gaba! from her distant past. "Do you think it'll come back?"

I look over at her and see the tape wrapped around her forearm holding a wad of cotton. "Will what come back?"

"My hair. 'Cause if it doesn't, I'm thinking about different things I could do."

"Yeah? Like what?"

"Maybe tattoos," she says.

This gives me pause, but I play along. "You could tattoo a map of the world so your head would be like a globe."

"Nooo." She laughs away my idea. "Hands. One on each side so it looks like someone is holding my head." I nod and like the idea of a permanent embrace. "Or eyes," she says. "I could have eyes tattooed on the back of my head. No one would stare at me that way."

"Are you sure about that?"

"When people stare, they always look away when they see you looking back at them."

"Normally, you have to become a parent before you get eyes in the back of your head," I say and smile.

Layla turns and looks out the window. I've gone too far into the future, planted the idea of a motherhood that may never be realized

We pull into the driveway and I push the button that opens the garage door. I park the car and turn off the ignition. "Okay, kiddo," I say and move to get out of the car, but Layla sits, holding the fabric in her lap, stroking it. I know she wants to say something, so I let my hand drop from the door handle. She never needs prodding when something is on her mind, so her reluctance means it's something serious.

Since her diagnosis, we have focused on treatment options, doctor's appointments, logistics. All small steps in the process. We keep things as tightly packed as possible, but occasionally things poke out. "Are you all right? Is the medicine getting to you?" She wants to nod, it seems to me—perhaps that's just wishful thinking—but her head tilts to the side and she looks at me. "I'm sad," she says. "About all this." She picks at the tape around her arm. "And about what's going to happen."

"Honey—"

"It's okay, Dad. You don't have to." She opens her door, gets out, and is inside the house before I have a chance to say anything. Karen has the same ability to disappear when she feels a conversation is over. It's a punctuation mark: a full stop, a dead battery you can't turn over.

I went to a lecture by an economist the other night. Going to a lecture, especially by an economist, is not something I usually do. But Layla was having a rough go that evening, nausea and such, and when a friend called and asked me if I wanted to go I said yes before I knew who the speaker was or what the topic of the talk would be about. I told Karen I had to do a favor for a friend. She looked at me and read the lie on my face but still nodded her assent.

The talk was about the economics of immigration and focused on the determinants each immigrant faces. She termed the factors as Push, Stay, Pull, and Stay Away. Push factors might be civil war or famine, while a Pull factors might be peace or personal freedom. "Each choice," she said, "is predicated on the perceived—not actual—costs associated with it." She used this model to explain aspects of the refugee crisis in Europe.

"Why," she asked, "do some choose to leave everything behind and forge into the unknown, risking their lives to cross the Mediterranean Sea, to risk starvation, assault, or indefinite internment in ill-equipped camps, to face the ridicule of xenophobic politicians?" She continued: "And why do some choose to stay amidst a warzone and suffer the ravages of brutal dictatorships or radical insurgents?"

It all boiled down to the survival of the family, no matter the personal cost. The choice to stay or go takes courage, a catastrophe possible with either option.

Her words echoed in my head as I tried to go to sleep that night. As a child, we never immigrated anywhere, but we did migrate. My father was a corporate gypsy. Whenever the word transferred popped up at the dinner table, I knew to expect a purge of toys and clothes, packing up everything else, and saying goodbye to friends, neighbors, and teachers.

"So long. It was nice knowing you," became a familiar refrain. I left the known and headed into the unknown many times.

Still, I had the stability of a family. My mother stayed home with me until I entered sixth grade. My father, when he wasn't traveling for business, ate at home every evening. My siblings tortured me on a regular basis, as any good sibling is supposed to do. And through all the moves, I always felt my parents knew best. It never got easy to say goodbye to the people we left behind, but I did learn how to do it.

When Karen and I discovered we were pregnant—yes, it was a surprise—we talked a lot about our childhoods and how we wanted to raise our child. Someone, we decided, would be a stay-at-home parent. That someone was me. Karen had the professional job with benefits; it was an easy choice.

In shops, I was the only guy carrying a diaper bag with an infant strapped to his chest, the only adult male at the playground, the lone father at the grocery store mid-morning pushing Layla in a race-car grocery cart. Mothers, at first surprised, would often comment on Layla's smile. It was a ruse. In their eyes I could see the desperate need for adult conversation, maybe even adult male conversation. We'd chat about the kids for a moment or two—asking about pediatricians or some new developmental toy, Leap Frog or something of the like—but then it'd turn more personal.

"You're so lucky to able have time with your daughter" and "Most men I know couldn't handle it for a day, let alone full-time," were repeated phrases. Invariably, it'd get around to, "So what does your wife do?" I was an open book to them. A stay-at-home dad, while initially interesting, was not much different from their own role. The real mystery, it seemed, was what Karen did. How did she escape? Is that the right word? Sometimes, though I didn't want to admit it, I felt the same curiosity.

Five weeks have passed and Layla is on her sixth round. As predicted by Dr. Bridges, her hair thinned considerably. While she is brushing it she stops and looks at her hand; a wispy ponytail hangs from it. I'd done my best to prepare her, but she is still surprised.

She drops the brush, goes to the bathroom, and shuts herself in. I expect to hear crying as I place my ear to the door, but all I can hear is the sound of water running. I wonder if she's picked up her mother's habit. Even after twenty years of marriage, whenever I'm around, Karen turns on the faucet every time she urinates.

Initially, I thought she was embarrassed by the sound, but now it seems more likely to be a physiological aid. I listen to the water and place my hand on the barrier between us. I want to speak to her through the door, to tell her it'll be all right, but I know I have to believe those things if there's any chance of convincing Layla.

Inside the bathroom, the water shuts off and I stand away from the door. I expect her to come out but nothing happens. I stand there so long I become self-conscious. The silence makes me imagine that she is no longer on the other side of the door, that she's left this world behind. As much as this imagined loss pains me, I can't help but think of what my life has meant over the last nine years. If she's gone, what would I have to show for all my time, effort, and love?

Would it mean anything to anybody?

I move away from the door, feeling embarrassed in an empty room. When she finally comes out, all of her hair is gone. Her bald head blazes in its sun-shy whiteness.

We are driving to another appointment

with Dr. Bridges. She's completed her last round of chemo and now we're hoping for good news. Layla is in the front passenger seat, though she's too young and too light if the airbag were to deploy. But I have trouble taking my eyes off her now. I stand in her doorway at night and watch her sleep, and I've set the hallway mirror up at an angle so I can peek down the hall and see her reading about Ramona Quimby in her beanbag chair. Though I could do the same with the rear-view mirror in the car, I prefer to keep her in my periphery, within arm's reach.

In front of the doctor's office sits a modern sculpture, a copper-colored orb of sorts; it's placed amidst a small rectangular greenspace formed by a white concrete retaining wall. Layla glances at it as we pass, but doesn't say anything. As we enter the doctor's office, people in the waiting room smile at the pink fuzzy hat she's fashioned. It's like a cloche, tight around her crown and a low slopping flair of a brim. She likes it because she can hide her eyes if she decides to. Once we're called back, I know it is bad news before Dr. Bridges says a word. He wears a smile that doesn't touch his eyes. He still isn't comfortable talking about Layla's prognosis with her in the room, but long ago she insisted. "It's happening to me," she said. "I have a right to know what's going on." Karen and I agreed, though Dr. Bridges wasn't enthusiastic about the idea.

"Well," he begins, keeping his eyes on me. "The numbers aren't looking so good."

"What's the next step?" Layla says before I have a chance.

Dr. Bridges adjusts himself in his seat. His elbows are on the desk and he holds his hands together as though he is making a church and steeple. He bows his head and touches the steeple to his lips. He lifts his eyes and looks at Layla for a moment and then to me. The way his fingers are laced, I can tell there are no people in the church.

"There is a trial," he says. "Layla might be a suitable candidate. But it is experimental." He's not optimistic. It's on his face. He's a man who's had this conversation before, telling parents a catastrophe is their new reality, and while he wants to extend some sort of confidence—to give the illusion at least—I can see it's hopeless. Still, I push forward. "What do you need us to do?" I ask.

"There are no guarantees," he says. I nod

and see Layla in my periphery. She's nodding too. We gave up the notion of guarantees the first time we visited the oncologist. Then she leans forward, pushing her hat back a bit so he can see her eyes.

"Even if it doesn't work for me, could it help someone else?" she asks.

"Perhaps," Dr. Bridges says.

We walk out of the doctor's office and the sun is setting. Layla takes off her hat and climbs up onto the retaining wall and walks through a little patch of grass to where the sculpture of the orb is mounted. The metallic sphere glows with end-of-the-day light. On one side it has a deep, concave portion, and at the center is a hole that goes all the way through. Layla buries her face in the cavity and peers into an undiscovered country. I see the back of her bald head, a bright white pupil in a dark eye.

"What do you see?" I ask. I wait, but she doesn't answer. I think about climbing up and looking at her face from the other side of the orb, just to be playful, but then I see her shoulders tremble, and I know she's crying. Her resolve through it all surpasses anything I could've maintained. As her tears drip from the bottom of the sculpture, I sit on the edge of the retaining wall and place her hat on my head, pulling the brim down to hide my eyes.

Nine months later, a package arrives. Too much life in the interim clouds my memory, and I don't recognize the return address. I open the small box and see two pendants. One is a dolphin, Layla's favorite animal. I ordered it for Karen, and now I'll have to be sure to mail it to her. The other is the size and shape of a quarter. The outer edge is ringed by oblong scales that surround a rostrum, a beaklike projection that looks like a clam shell or a closed eye. It's a barnacle sculpted by a jeweler from compressed cremains. I pick it up and am surprised by its heft. I run a colored string through the silver eyelet at the top and place it around my neck. After a moment, I move the pendant around. The cord feels like it might be choking me, in a feeble sort of way, but the weight on my back feels good.

The Accountant in 5E

Larry the dog didn't live with people. Well, not in the same house with people. He lived on his own in a small flat on the Lower East Side of Manhattan, a nice address overlooking the East River. Although he enjoyed his work as an accountant, the city left him wanting. Watching the sun rise and cast its glow upon the water each morning helped him through each urban day. Seeing its persistence gave him strength and mollified his need to be surrounded by nature. He'd visited Central Park a few times when he first moved to New York, but the leash law had caused more than one embarrassing situation with the police. And he did enjoy the occasional visit to the tiny neighborhood parks, but these small oases never provided the full emersion into nature he so desired. As a dog, and he was a dog, life in the city was not easy for Larry.

One night a neighbor, Blair Abbey, invited him to a cocktail party. He had seen her before in the foyer of the apartment building when they were both retrieving their mail. She was a short and slight woman with mannerisms that reminded Larry of the flightiness of a bird. Few words had been exchanged between them since he'd moved into the building, so the invitation had been unexpected, though not entirely unwelcomed.

It is surprisingly easy to feel lonely amidst the millions in the city.

The party was at the home of Blair's friend who worked with the Greenwich Village Society for Historic Preservation, so many of the guests were benefactors of the arts district. On the whole, the crowd was warm and welcoming to Larry, though he did feel a bit socially awkward. Many of the conversation topics referenced artists he'd never heard of or issues within the arts community he lacked enough knowledge about to offer any meaningful contribution. He simply wore a placid face and nodded.

At cocktail parties he didn't like to show his teeth—humans can easily get skittish. Nodding was helpful in the human world, but sometimes he felt like he resembled those toy dogs on the back dash of cars bouncing their heads up and down with each bump in the road. Eventually, Larry was introduced to a fellow accountant who worked for Deloitte & Touche. After a few glasses of wine and a lively conversation about credit default swaps and the potential downfall of AIG, Larry loosened up. He was laughing and enjoying himself as Blair and he stood arm in arm, the differences between he and the rest of the guests having melted away.

The accountant from Deloitte & Touche leaned in with a serious expression and asked, "Can I give you a bit of life advice?"

Larry nodded, unsure of what was to come.

The accountant's eyes darted around the room indicating a gravity to what he was about to utter. "If you're ever attacked by a group of clowns, be sure to go for the juggler."

The joke tickled Larry more than he expected and though he was not much of a tail wager at this moment his tail took on a life of its own and he knocked a glass of wine onto the host's expensive Persian rug. And, of course, it was red wine.

If he'd been human, Larry's embarrassment would've been displayed on his face with a rise in color, but as a dog, his shame manifested in his tail curling under, tucking itself between his hind legs.

"It's okay, Larry," Blair said. "It wouldn't be a party unless there was a spill."

But seeing his host on her knees blotting up his mess made him feel like a puppy who'd yet to be housetrained. No matter how many apologies he offered or how many times the hostess tried to dismiss his concerns, Larry still felt devastated. He and Blair left the party shortly afterward and spoke few words on the cab ride home. Once back at their apartment building, Larry shook hands with Blair and after thanking her for the evening, excused himself, and returned to his apartment alone.

Later that night, his neighbors heard loud noises coming from his apartment. Several described it as baleful howls. Now Larry kept his place clean, did his own shopping and cooking, never played his TV or stereo too loud, served as a conscientious member of the co-op board, and like any accountant worth his salt, always paid his rent on time. Overall, he was a good tenant and a fine neighbor. Still, this howling business had many of his neighbors concerned and over the next several days many conversations addressed the issue.

"It sounds so sad," Blair Abby from 5C said.

"I wonder if it's sexual," Molly from 5F mused.

"It's a seasonal thing. I remember hearing it last spring," Ms. Blank in 5G said.

The night in question, the very night of the party, Larry had curled up in the middle of his king-sized bed. His nose twitched as if it had landed upon an ancient scent, his eyes worked furiously behind closed lids, and the muscles in his paws flexed in and out. In his dream he is alone in the woods under a dense canopy in fading light. Delightfully complex fungi, benign moss, sharp pine needles, and the tantalizing rot of millions of leaves curl through his canine proboscis. Larry walks on all fours in the dream, his nose mere millimeters from the earth smelling all this and rabbits, squirrels, birds, and one cunning fox who had traipsed through the area recently. He is in his element, following the trail of something long passed and hidden.

Silver and gold cuts of light begin to dance on the trunks of the trees as the sun sets, and Larry makes his way to the edge of a vast meadow with a small snaking creek at its center.

A glowing moon, larger than possible, sits on the horizon. Something primal stirs deep within him. Yearning, loneliness, and an ache ball up and pulse from a place below his heart. He opens his mouth and these feelings fly into the night as in his canine song. In his dream, Larry is himself, he is able to express his nature.

He didn't hear the howls that night because he was too busy feeling them, and, upon waking, Larry didn't remember a thing, though he did feel refreshed. As he left his apartment and went to work, he wore his placid face as usual, always mindful of how humans might react. Some call it a dog eat dog world, but for Larry, it was more of a human kill dog world. One needs to look no further than the shoulders of highways or animal shelters to realize this.

On his way to work the next morning, Larry took a slight detour and strolled through his neighborhood park, the type with stonewalls and gothic wrought iron gates. He walked along the path and took in the green richness of the grass and the other aromas floating through the air. It was a fine respite from all the exhaust fumes spewed on the streets. Larry felt good, but then he passed an elderly woman walking an equally elderly terrier. While cocktail parties were treacherous in abiding social mores, his neighborhood park had its own snares. The terrier, Olly the woman called him, was a persistent individual who hung onto old ways and insisted upon a traditional greeting. The ancient terrier stood on his hind legs and placed his cold nose firmly against Larry's behind. The woman was apologetic and pulled hard on Olly's leash. Once Olly was gone, Larry felt both relief and something else. Something akin to the feeling one has when a ritual is interrupted or left incomplete.

A few weeks after the howling incident the co-op called a meeting to address the tenants' concerns. Of course, they didn't want to offend Larry, so they scheduled the meeting while he was at work. You might surmise that they actually didn't care about his feelings at all, but rather they were simply scared by what "this crazy dog" might do.

Larry worked as a CPA at Smith, Barney & Wilcox and it was tax season. April 15th fell on a Sunday this particular year, so the IRS extended the tax deadline until Tuesday the 17th. The tenants scheduled the meeting for the 17th knowing Larry would be working late helping people file, or, as Walter from 6E suggested, "Creating a shell company to hide revenue from the IRS or a future ex-spouse."

Ms. Blank from 5G spoke first. "I think we all agree that there is a problem."

Those in attendance murmured their affirmation.

"And something needs to be done about it," she continued. Ms. Blank's concerns about property values made her apprehensive about allowing Larry to sign a lease in the first place.

The tenants shared sheepish glances with one another and reluctantly nodded in consent.

Walter from 6E, directly above Larry's apartment, stood up. "So what are we going to do about it? I can't lose another night's sleep. I'm a subway operator. You don't want me sleepy when I'm on the job."

Molly from 5F, who lived directly across the hall from Larry, chimed in. "I'm afraid to invite people over. What are they going to say when they hear that awful noise?"

But Blair Abby of 5C came to Larry's defense. "Listen to yourselves," she said. "This is Larry we're talking about. Larry who's been our friend and neighbor for a while now. Walter, I know he helped you dig your garden in the courtyard. And Molly, I can't say I've noticed any decrease in the frequency of your guests, especially late-night traffic. And if I'm being honest, I may have heard a bit of howling coming from your side of the hallway as well."

Molly paled as people chuckled and then she reddened.

"And Ms. Blank, we all know you and Larry haven't gotten along since the incident with Mr. Whiskers, but that's been months. I have to say I'm surprised to see the lengths you're willing to go." Blair looked over the tenants, meeting only the few eyes that were willing to meet hers.

While Larry's neighbors debated his suitability as a tenant in their building, Larry was assessing his own place at work. He felt certain breeds are adept at particular skills or have specific qualities. For instance, Rottweilers are muscular, loyal, and not afraid to attack, and Labradors don't flinch at the sound of a gun. If

Larry worked for the mob, being a Rottweiler or a Labrador would've been a good match between disposition and profession. And while Larry was a capable CPA, he felt his skill set better matched that of a forensic accountant. He was tenacious, plodding, smart, and he could follow a scent. He'd even applied for such a position within Smith Barney & Wilcox, but his efforts had yet to bear fruit.

That day, as he pondered his future in his cubicle, he and his fellow CPAs were introduced to the new Junior Accounts Manager, Chad. The position came with an office, which left Larry's considerable nose a bit out of joint. Chad took the time to come by and meet each CPA, but after few minutes of conversation, Larry decided Chad had the IQ of a pineapple and the social grace of a DMV employee. After he introduced himself all Chad said was, "Bloodhound, huh?"

"Yes," Larry said. "So you were transferred from corporate headquarters?"

Chad just smiled and nodded. Stupid human, Larry thought. Chad should be on a back dash of a car somewhere. A transfer away from corporate HQ was never a good thing, even if you do get an office out of the deal. Larry figured the biped would be gone within the year or maybe prompted to upper management. It was hard to tell with humans

There were times he wondered how humans could've ended up in charge of everything. Dogs were superior in every way. Dogs can run faster, smell and hear better, were inherently loyal, honest, and had the instinct to protect the ones they cared about. You couldn't say the same thing about most humans. As Larry finished up for the day, he took stock of all he'd done since lunch: post-dated an IRA withdrawal, reconciled Swiss bank account statements for two clients, completed four 1040s, opened an off-shore account for a client, submitted sixteen 1090s, and filed a 990 for a 501 c3 he was doing pro bono work for, a no-kill animal shelter in Queens. Satisfied with his work, he headed home.

As he walked into the foyer of the apartment building, he stopped to check his mail. An envelope from Smith, Barney & Wilcox was the only item in the narrow mailbox. He opened it, slid out the contents, and his jaw dropped. It was then that he overheard a familiar voice.

"Would we even be having this meeting if Larry wasn't a dog?" Blair said. "Has anyone even spoken to him about the howling?" Larry edged to the door that was slightly ajar and listened.

"How do you bring up something like that?" Walter asked. "I mean, it could be sexual. I don't want to give him the wrong impression." Walter chuckled and a few people joined in.

"Larry's straight, Walter. I know for sure," Blair said.

Walter arched his eyebrows. "You know for sure, huh?"

"We dated. Well, we went on a date. He had a bit too much to drink but was still a perfect gentleman." Blair folded her arms.

"I bet he was. He's ever so mannerly," Walter said. He smiled, but the distance between him and the others began to grow.

"So he should've taken advantage of me? Is that what you're trying to say, Walter?"

Walter's head sunk between his shoulders. His mouth moved, but nothing intelligible came out, just a stuttering "I—I—I"

And then Larry walked into the meeting

room. He showed a slow, gentle wag to his neighbors. "Sorry, I'm late to the meeting. Somehow it didn't make it onto my planner. Tax season, you know. Lots of things slip through the cracks."

No one said anything.

"It's a joke, an accounting joke. We don't let anything slip through the cracks."

Blair, with her arms still folded turned to Walter, who by this point was slouching in his seat. "Walter, would you like to tell Larry about the details of this meeting?" Walter acted as though he hadn't heard and rubbed his palms together.

"What's going on?" Larry asked.

"Larry, there have been some disturbances," said Walter.

"And?"

"Several of the tenants, your neighbors— well, are troubled by the sounds coming from your apartment."

"This meeting is about me? That's why I didn't know about it?" Larry did his best to keep from showing his teeth. It was so rare to see Walter, normally condescending and self-righteous, squirm like a puppy who just wet the rug. Larry stopped the gentle wag of his tail and curled it under a bit, which took considerable effort given his elated mood. He looked at each of his neighbors with his big, ever-so-sincere, brown eyes. No one returned his gaze. In his mind he envisioned himself wagging a paw at them all and saying Bad Humans.

"I told them to talk to you," Blair said.

"Why didn't you talk to me? He asked.

Blair's head dropped as her indignation seemed to slip into embarrassment.

Larry stood there and decided to count to thirty before saying anything else. This was something that he'd picked up at work. Sometimes he'd have clients who were hiding something. Technically, all his clients were trying to hide something, but they couldn't hide it from their accountant. That was a deal breaker. So on those occasions when his nose told him something was amiss, he'd simply say, "And anything else?"

He'd give them the long, thirty-second stare. They normally crumbled around the fifteen to twenty-second mark. But tonight, he didn't need any more information. He had everything he needed. It was a matter of retribution at this point. All those side-eye glances, the way they'd held their newspapers a bit tighter as he walked by, and all the "good boy" and snide remarks they'd made over the months. They were all damned speciesists.

When he reached thirty, he cleared his throat and addressed his neighbors. "Before I walked in the air was filled with the musk of conquest, but now it's soured with fear and shame." Larry tapped his nose. "It's hard to hide the acrid smell of deceit."

"Larry," Blair said. Larry held up his paw.

"Anyway," he said and pulled out the envelope from Smith, Barney & Wilcox. "I'll be gone in a couple of the months. I've been promoted and transferred to the corporate office in San Francisco. Seems someone values my instincts, loyalty, and attention to detail. They think I'll make a fine forensic accountant."

Larry returned the letter to his breast pocket, thought about the promise of his new position, which included a bayside condo in Sausalito and the option to telecommute two days a week, and walked out of the meeting, giving his neighbors a liberal wag of his tail as he departed.

As the sound of his footfalls faded, the neighbors turned to one another in dismay. Then a growing sound, like that of a teakettle coming to a boil, rang through the building. A howl resonating with joy and triumph rattled their bones and left them wondering if they might have handled the situation in a more neighborly way. But as humans, and they were human, the moment of self-reflection quickly passed. "He'll be gone soon enough," Walter said, and the rest of the tenants agreed, put Larry out of their mind, and moved onto other co-op business.

Westport

Beyond the inlet to Grays Harbor, still in the waters of the Pacific, a trawler puts in for home. Diesel exhaust rises and dissipates over the small boat as it rides the choppy waves of the open ocean. In the distance, I can see the line that separates the wild of the sea from the tame of the harbor. The boarder is marked not only in a difference in turbulence but also in a shift of color from slate grey to a murky green that reminds me of the moss that grows on the north sides of trees near my home.

I don't remember ever having seen the ocean before. I was two when my Mom and I moved away from Westport to a small town in western Montana. Occasionally, Washington would come up in some conversation and I'd see something change. Like a storm brewing, her eyes would change from a steel blue to a cold gray. She'd wall off part of herself and I knew better than to try to gain entry to the land of her secrets. Afterward, once she felt less threatened, she'd try to make things up to me with bribes of sweets or clothes. I never understood how a person could be so opaque and utterly transparent at the same time.

Over the last year or so it wasn't hard to figure out something was wrong with her, something bad. She tried to keep it to herself, to protect me I suppose, but she couldn't hide the doctor's appointments all the way up in Helena, and when she said the word cancer, I understood. Despite their best efforts, the doctors couldn't do anything to save her. She passed in a hospice bed, her head wrapped in a silk scarf, and her eyes sunken so deeply into her face it was like she was falling away while perfectly still.

Mother's Day had always been a big deal in

our home. Me, my Mom, and my grandma always got together and celebrated. They would tell stories from childhood and of motherhood, and they'd tell me what a fine mother I would be some day. Not surprisingly, Father's Day was the opposite. Grandma's husband sought his fortune up in the Yukon and left her alone and pregnant with my mother. Mom never talked about my father, and I was sure he'd committed some grave act to make her leave Westport. But on that Sunday in June each year, I always felt questions rising up inside, but I never had the nerve to ask.

After mom passed, grandma and I cleaned out her things, and I found a shoebox on the top shelf of her closet. A maroon ribbon that reminded me of the color of dried blood tied the box shut. Inside the box were dozens of letters and postcards going back to the year we moved to Montana. Grandma tried to wrest the box from me. "That's private," she'd said. I elbowed her out of the way and locked myself in the bathroom and read them all. They were from him, my father. I traced my fingers along the lines and swoops of the words he wrote and felt indentations when he pushed hard on the pen and small mountains of dried ink at the points where he paused for thought.

I didn't get the answers I was looking for. Each note either apologized or pleaded, but never said what for. In the last letter that came, maybe a year or so ago, he included a picture of a fishing boat he bought. He wrote he named her Nellie, after me. The tone in the last letter was different. He'd stopped apologizing and pleading for forgiveness, and even stopped asking for a chance to see me. He said he understood things were never going to go back to the way they were, that they'd both moved on with their lives, and that it was simply too painful to try to hang onto to something that he could never have. At the end of the letter he wrote, "For love, I'll disappear."

I stand on a dock in Westport with the evening wind blowing on my face. I'm not sure what I'll find here, but something called and I had to answer. The trawler chugs up to the dock and sooty clouds hang in the air high overhead, blending into the blue-gray sky. I take a step and smell the ocean and an embrace what feels like home. The wind gusts and I think I hear someone call my name.

Finale

I look through the window and see the piano movers waiting, leaning against the hydraulic lift on the back of the truck with cigarettes dangling from their mouths, and then I turn away. My grandmother's hands dance a ragtime rhythm and she nods punctuation at the end of each musical phrase. Her fingers, bent with age and arthritis, jump octaves with ease. She knuckles some high notes and rides a glissando down the keyboard. The music stops and reverberates off the bare walls and through the empty house.

She sits for a moment, looking at the keys. Her shoulders rise a bit as she inhales, and it seems like she's about to say something but doesn't. She reaches up and drops the fall and runs her hand across the polished wood like she's soothing a thoroughbred.

"I'm ready, Jack," she says.

It's my grandfather's name she uses to address me, but I don't correct her. Now's not the time to explain. I place my hand under her elbow and help her up from the bench and we make our way to the door. Her steps are short but steady. I open the door and help her through. We stand on the porch a moment as she looks out across the yard. The piano movers straighten up and ditch their cigarettes.

I give them a nod.

As we descend the steps, she pats my hand and says, "You're a good grandson, Peter."

I open the passenger door and she sits and places her purse square in her lap. I pull the seatbelt down so she doesn't have to reach around. She takes the buckle and looks at me. "At this point, I don't think it really matters." Her finger releases it and a hidden spring reels in the slack. I start to say something, but I know everything I could possibly think to say she's already heard at some point in her eighty years. So I close the door and walk around to the other side of the car.

"Your grandfather would've never owned a Japanese car. He built planes during the war to shoot those peckers down."

I nod. The Grumman Wildcat FM2 was built by General Motors, and my grandfather oversaw their production as a line manager at the Turnstedt Division in New Jersey. Mitsubishi built the A6M Zero, the planes with blood red circles on their wings and fuselage that strafed seamen at Pearl Harbor and other islands in the South Pacific during WWII. I drive a Honda, built by a company that wasn't founded until 1948, but I don't mention this.

I put the car in reverse and as we pull away I see the piano movers in my rearview mirror buckle their back support belts and make their way toward the house. My grandmother looks out the passenger window of the car and watches the homes of her neighbors drift by for the last time. Her knuckles turn white as the grip on her purse tightens.

"Mom wanted to know if she could bring you anything."

She doesn't say a word, and then she shakes her head. "Isn't that sweet of her."

At the end of the street, I turn onto White Horse Avenue and pass Blackstone's Dinner, the restaurant my grandfather took me for breakfast when I came to visit as a child. We drive a bit farther and I see a sign for Dunham's, the department store my grandmother worked at for three decades. I recognize the name from the gift boxes filled with dress shirts and slacks sent every Christmas.

"She knows this isn't easy for you," I say.

My grandmother nods. And then she looks at me with eyes like a sharpshooter. "Seems to me she's making it easy on herself sending you along to fetch me."

Several things run through my mind and as each tries to escape through my mouth I clench my teeth and keep them captive. We take the entrance to the Turnpike and I accelerate into the flow of traffic. Cars cluster at 80 mph. The man driving the Cadillac next to me is holding a folded newspaper on the steering wheel with his thumb and a cell phone in the other hand. A light rain begins to fall and I turn on the windshield wipers.

"Forest Manor sounds more like a cemetery than a nursing home."

"Mom says it's an assisted living facility. The best in the state."

"It's a place people only leave when they're dead. Call it what you will."

I change lanes and keep the distracted Cadillac driver in front of me, careful to watch for brake lights in front of him. "Mom says they have a piano."

She rubs her knuckles and looks out the window. "Your grandfather bought me my piano in 1946 with a bonus check from GM. I haven't touched the ivories on another one since then."

My instructions were simple. My mother said, "Take your grandmother by her house after the movers have boxed and removed all her belongings. Make sure the piano movers are scheduled for 1:00, arrive ten minutes late, tip them twenty dollars each and ask them to wait for another fifteen minutes while she plays a few tunes. Bring her to Forest Manor afterward to meet us so we can show her the apartment. Do you think you can handle that?"

We come up on the Gordon Road exit and my grandmother says, "Get off here."

"That's not—"

"You're going to miss it."

I change lanes and a car honks. I exit and see a sign for Princeton Memorial Park, the cemetery where my grandfather is buried.

"Turn left." I nod and follow her directions.

I try to help her as she walks through the grass to her husband's grave, but she shakes off my hand. I slow and let her walk ahead alone.

When she reaches the gravesite, she places her hand on the tombstone and looks skyward. Her mouth moves but I'm too far away to hear what she says. I check my watch and can imagine my mother's impatient foot tapping as she waits for us at Forest Manor. But I don't rush.

My grandfather passed away over twenty years ago. He suffered a stroke in a library and landed on a pile of books about space travel and continental drift. Unseen by anyone for far too long, the ischemic cascade robbed him of his essence. After a week in the hospital, he succumbed quietly amidst the beeping and whir of an automated heart and blood pressure monitor. My grandmother was there when he passed.

A week later, she was in the same hospital with a broken hip and a concussion after falling down the stairs to the basement. She was found by a neighbor who she often suspected of spying and eavesdropping. In the hospital, she pointed to her rescue as proof that her accusations were well-founded and that she was indeed not paranoid.

My grandmother drops to her knees and I move toward her, but I realize she's praying and stay back. The wind gusts and rustles the leaves on the trees and floats strands of gray hair from her head. After a few minutes I move in and rest my hand on her shoulder. She crosses herself and I help her up. We walk back to the car in silence, arm in arm.

Back on the Turnpike, we are only a few exits away from Forest Manor. She looks at me and I know something is on her mind. "What is it?"

"Take me to the shore."

"Mom and Dad are waiting for us."

"Your grandfather would be so proud of you. He was a company man, too."

I turn and she's looking straight ahead with her hands on her purse. She's not focused on anything, just looking out onto the road as if it were a blank slate waiting to be filled. She pulls a tissue from the cuff of her jacket sleeve and dabs her eyes and then replaces it. She does not sniffle or plead.

We pass the Jamesburg exit and she reaches over and pats my shoulder. "Keansburg," she says.

Moments later, as if she had sight of my car

and watched me pass the exit for Forest Manor, my mother rings my phone. I look at the picture that accompanies her number. She's in a business suit, sitting on the corner of her office desk with a rolled document in her hand. The photo came from her business' website. I hit ignore and put the phone back in my pocket and accelerate into the passing lane. The phone rings six more times in the next thirty minutes. I don't answer any of the calls.

We pull into the public beach at Keansburg and my grandmother gets out of the car before I have a chance to put it in park. "Wait here," she says as she closes the door.

I sit for a moment and watch her disappear behind a dune. My phone rings again and I look to see who it is, though I already know. I think about hitting the ignore button, but then let the phone ring until it goes to voicemail. There'll be hell to pay, but I know these are the last moments of freedom my grandmother will ever experience. From here on there will be orderlies and nurses and doctors and activity directors and fellow residents encroaching on her world. These moments on the shore have to last her until the end.

My phone rings again. "Christ." I struggle
with the seatbelt and get out of the car. The sky
is gray and the wind and the tide are coming in.
The sea air pelts my face with bits of sand and
salt as I make my way over the barrier dunes. I
see my grandmother's sensible shoes
abandoned in the sand and footprints left by her
bare feet. Ahead, she is walking into the surf.
Flotsam swirls and her dark dress ripples in the
wind until a wave crashes and pastes the fabric
to her body and legs. She staggers under the
weight of the water but remains upright. I slog
through the sand to reach her. The water cedes
the beach and she drops her purse into the
retreating water. It tumbles across the sand and
floats into the wash, vanishing under the break
of the next wave.

I decide to run and push off. The ground
melts away under my feet and I take another
step before I've gotten anywhere with the first
one. My arms pump the air and my legs churn
the sand in a frenzy, all with no effect.
Expectations—my mother's, my grandmother's,
and my own—trip me and I fall face first into
the sand, grit, and salt.

She turns back to me and raises a hand. I
see her smile in a way she does only when she

has let go of herself. Those times when she is lost in the world of a book, when she tells stories about before she was married, or when she becomes the music of a song and the rhythm moves her body and her hands dance across the keys of a piano.

No Safe Harbor

We had just returned from a spaghetti dinner at church when everything went to hell. Mama and Dad had fights all the time, but this one was different. Mama insisted Dad was flirting with Miss Carla, the pastor's wife. Dad said that Mama wanted to ride Mr. Bob, one of the deacons in the church, like a pogo-stick, or something like that. Then it was as if Jesus tapped them on the shoulder because they stopped arguing and looked at me.

"Get to bed," Dad said.

I didn't hesitate, and the arguing didn't stop. I heard one word clearly—Joe.

Joe was Mama's older brother. He lived near New Orleans and owned a shrimp boat. When I heard his name, I knew what Mama was going to do. I decided I was going to stow away, and so I packed my knapsack. I tried to figure out a way to get it in the trunk of the car without them seeing me. The only choice was to sneak past their bedroom, but with the mood Dad was in— Instead, I buried my head under the pillow and waited for it to stop.

Sometime later, my bedroom door opened. I saw Mama's silhouette in the doorway; the hall lights were on so I couldn't see her face.

"Where are you going?"

She'd seen the knapsack. I tried but couldn't answer. Mama walked over and sat on the edge of my bed, and I reached out and hugged her, pressing my face against her midsection. In her arms, I felt safe, as though nothing or no one could harm me.

"It'll be okay."

I don't know what she said to Dad after she left my room, but the next morning we left for Uncles Joe's. Mama let me sit in the front seat with her. As we turned onto the street Mama looked over at me and said, "Are you ready for an adventure?"

At the top of her arm, I could see four fat lines that looked like fingers. I was about to ask her about them when she reached over and turned on the radio. "Sweet Caroline" burst out of the speakers and we sang along as we drove away.

By early afternoon, we were near New Orleans. We drove over a huge bridge that crossed the Mississippi and landed us in St. Bernard parish. Uncle Joe lived on Bayou Dupre, a little community just off a canal that runs between the Mississippi and Lake Borgne. We traveled down a narrow road atop a levee to where Uncle Joe docked his boat. Mama said he was more likely to be there than home.

We turned into the entrance of the tiny harbor; small white shells dredged from the bottom of the lake crunched under the tires in the parking lot. The boats rocked gently in their slips, and lines beat against the steel booms that held trawling nets hoisted above the decks. Seagulls swayed from side to side in the air as though tethered with a kite string. I felt a strange stillness in the car. The absence of the sound of the engine made it seem like something was missing. It was peaceful, but I felt something else with it. Kind of how keeping secrets can make you feel special and lonely at the same time.

After Mama had parked, she stared off into the distance, hanging onto the steering wheel as if she were still driving. I followed her eyes to the emptiness of the horizon. A gentle wind pushed through the open windows and rustled her hair.

"Can I get out?"

She nodded, and I jumped out of the car and ran toward the dock. A large pelican sat perched on an old creosote pole. The bird looked at me with his large gray eyes and spread his wings as I ran by. My Keds pounded on the sun-bleached slats that separated me from the green water.

“Be careful,” Mama called.

Down the bayou a shrimp boat chugged along the calm water. The boat rode low in the water under the weight of its catch. The curve of the bow and the leading edge of the keel sliced through the calm water, and the wake rippled outward in a V and lapped against the dock under my feet.

I searched up and down the canal for Uncle Joe's boat. The sun was setting and the line that separated sea and the sky was becoming faint. I turned and looked back at Mama, who sat in the car with the windows open. Her reddish-brown hair drifted across her face and she smoothed it away. I could tell something was weighing upon her.

At the end of the dock, there was a boat moored next to another creosote post. On the boat was an old shrimper. His hands were busy darning the mass of green nylon netting piled between his white boots. I waved and he nodded. When I reached the post, seagulls took to the safety of the sky and peered at me with their small black eyes. I wrapped my arm around the pole and lowered one foot down to the green water, trying to set my foot on it.

The swells moved too fast and my foot was under and then above the water quicker than I could adjust. I wondered how Jesus could walk on water if it wouldn't stay still. On that thought, my fingers slipped from the post and I fell in.

I tried to pop back up, but my head hit something slimy and solid. Above me, air bubbles formed a liquid mirror. I was caught up under the dock. My chest began to rise and fall as my body hungered for air. I kicked my legs and pounded the underside of the dock. In a panic, I opened my mouth to yell and water rushed in, and then things faded.

When I opened my eyes, I was on my side; water spewed from my mouth as my stomach convulsed. I coughed. More water came out and made me wince. I lay on my back on the dock, and my mother's long hair dripped water on my face. Her eyes were wide and white in the shadow of her face. I heard the seagulls squawking. It sounded like laughter. I closed my eyes.

She shook me. "Jerry! Are you okay?"

She wrapped her arms around my neck and hugged me, burying my face in her wet hair. I smelled the bayou water and my stomach lurched. I didn't want her to let go of me, but I pushed her away and wretched again.

"He'll be alright," I heard a man's voice say. "Just a little waterlogged."

The shrimper who had been mending his nets stood behind my mother. His wet black hair pressed tight on his head like a stocking cap and his wide belly pushed out against his soaked white t-shirt.

"I don't know how to thank you," she said.

"Tain't nothin', ma'am."

She picked me up and carried me. The warmth of the day had slipped away, and I could feel her shivering.

"Sorry," I said.

She looked at me and tried to smile. She put me in the front seat of the car and got an old blanket from the trunk. The coarse cloth made my skin itchy. My Keds were wet, and I felt little puddles underneath my toes. She got in the car and began to dig in her purse. I looked out past the dock, hoping to see Uncle Joe's boat.

"Goddamnit!" she said.

"Sorry, Mama."

She shook her head. "I can't find my keys."

She kept digging and I kept hoping to see Uncle Joe's boat. If I could just see it come back to the harbor, I knew everything would be alright. He'd know what to do. I could imagine him laughing off the accident. His smile would melt the worry we were so tightly wrapped in.

"Jesus Christ! Where the hell are they?"

I looked over at the ignition and pointed. She didn't see me right away, but I held my arm outstretched. When she saw the keys dangling in the ignition, she began to laugh. I smiled. She really thought it was funny. And then—I couldn't tell exactly when it changed—she began crying. She banged her hands on the steering wheel, hitting the horn like exclamation marks. The old shrimper glanced back over his shoulder at us. She stopped beating the horn, rested her head against the top of the steering wheel, and sobbed. I reached out to her and she pushed my hand away and pounded the front dash. Puffs of dust kicked up in the fading sun. She grabbed me and pulled me to her. It scared me at first, but she buried her face in my shoulder and cried, heaving at times, holding me very tight. Her warm breath went right through the blanket and goose bumps prickled my skin.

It got dark and Mama gave up on waiting for Uncle Joe. We drove to a small motel, got out of our wet clothes, and cleaned up. For dinner, she took me to a roadside diner. We sat in a booth that had its own little jukebox. "Sweet Caroline" was one of the selections, but we didn't play it. Mama let me get a cheeseburger, fries, and a chocolate shake. My food came on wax paper in a little red basket. She sat there and watched me eat.

"You want a fry?" I held one up to her and she shook her head.

"I just need some coffee to warm my bones," she said.

I saw her hands shaking, even though she tried to hide it. I took another bite of my cheeseburger and my stomach rumbled. I still had some of that bayou water in me. I brushed my forearm across my forehead and sighed.

"You don't have to finish, honey. Just eat what you can," she said. I nodded and took another fry for good measure.

We went back to the motel after dinner and Mama tried calling Uncle Joe. She stood, wrapping the phone cord around her fingers. There was no answer and she returned the handset to the cradle, letting her hand rest on it for a moment. I thought she might try calling Dad next, but instead she turned on the TV and sat on the bed next to me. The long day hit me all of a sudden. The bed was hard and the springs squeaked every time I moved, but my eyes were heavy and I drifted off to the sounds of laughter from the TV.

Sometime during the night, I heard sirens. The dark room glowed orange. I got out of bed and pulled aside the curtains. Across from the motel, a house was ablaze. Firetrucks were in the middle of the street with lights flashing and firefighters pulling hoses. I could feel the heat

through the window and saw a mama with her
two kids, a boy and a girl. She held onto to them
tightly, one on either side. The little girl had a
stuffed animal of some sort that she held to her
face as she twisted from side to side under her
mama's arm. They were all in their pajamas.
Arcs of water curved into the house and orange
cinders streaked through the black smoke.
There was a commotion and the firemen
hollered. Then the roof collapsed and the house
fell in on itself. Sparks and embers filled the sky.
Just then, I felt Mama's hand on my shoulder.
"Good Lord," she said.

The next morning, we packed up the car.
Across the street were the remains of the home
that had caught fire. I stood there for a long
moment.

"The important thing is everyone got out,
honey," Mama said.

"But where will they go?"

"I'm sure they have family they can stay
with," she said.

The black jagged beams that had held up
the roof looked like a pile of burnt toothpicks.
How something so fragile looking could have
ever been so sturdy was a mystery. At the front

of the pile was a concrete stoop that led to a door no longer there. The charred chimney still stood at one end, like a lonely finger pointing skyward. We stood there in the parking lot for a long time, just looking to where it pointed.